D0667076

The Holy Terror

FRANÇOIS MAURIAC

The Holy Terror

DRAWINGS BY INGRID FETZ

FUNK & WAGNALLS
A Division of Reader's Digest Books, Inc.
NEW YORK

The Holy Terror

One

"Excuse me, is this the right train for Millasse?"

The fat man in the third-class compartment had already noticed the speaker, a small, shabby-looking young woman, as she got out of the express and struggled awkwardly with two heavy suitcases.

"It had better be the train for Millasse because that's where I'm going myself. In fact I live in Millasse. You'll be all right here. You've got some pretty heavy bags, though — I doubt if they'll go on the rack. Still, there's plenty of room on the seat . . . ."

He hoisted the newcomer's luggage into the carriage and then sat back, mopping his scarlet face, while he studied her more closely. She was dressed in a neat but well-worn suit and her gloves showed signs of frequent washing. The cheap, chain-store hat was almost jaunty by comparison and her shoes looked new.

All the same, she was definitely what the fat man called a lady. Why on earth could she be going to Millasse? He leaned his huge bulk forward and stared boldly into the stranger's pale face, making no attempt to hide his curiosity.

"So you're going to Millasse?"

"Yes."

"Got relations there, I expect?"

"No."

"Can't be going there for fun. Millasse is no joke — you have to be born there. You're on business, then?"

"Not exactly."

"You wouldn't be the new schoolteacher by any chance?"

"No."

"All the same, I can tell you're an educated person."

She nodded vaguely and looked out the window as the little train moved off, determined to put an end to this interrogation. But she did not know Loucrocq.

"With all that luggage — I mean, you must be meaning to stay for some time?"

She indicated, without taking her eyes from the window, that this was the case. It was a fine evening in early September; the workers in the vineyards straight-

ened up to watch the train, and children waved hand-
kerchiefs. A cart piled high with baskets of black grapes
stood waiting at a grade crossing. Already there were
pine trees here and there between the vineyards.

"You're a commercial traveller, perhaps?"

Pretending to take the lady's silence for assent, he
went on:

"You'll do all right if you put up at Benquey's. I hear
it's quite clean but, of course, I've had no call to find
out for myself: as I told you, I belong in Millasse — a
butcher, like my poor father before me. You'll see our
house in the square. But there's nothing wrong with the
food at Benquey's. Mother Benquey's stews are famous
for miles around. But don't be taken in by their wine —
it's all the same as what you get with their cheaper
meals. Benquey's hotel isn't in the square, you know,
and it's not easy to find on a dark night. I'll take you
there."

"Thank you, but I am not going to the hotel. I am
being met at the station." With this she opened her bag
and took out a newspaper; but if she thought she had
put off Loucrocq she soon found out her mistake.

"So you've come to stay with someone, then? It
wouldn't be the new parson? They say he has a sister
. . . is that it?"

This could not go on. The lady thought a word
would be enough to satisfy her tormentor.

"I am going to live with Monsieur Chevalier."

"With Monsieur Chevalier?"

"Yes. I am the new governess."

She picked up her paper again, but Loucrocq's obvious astonishment made her curious.

"Well now, who'd have thought it!" he brayed, slapping his thighs with two ham-like hands. "The new governess, eh? Oh dear, oh dear! So you're going to saddle yourself with Ernest? You poor little thing!"

She had given up any idea of breaking off the conversation.

"Why poor? I have been assured that they are very good people, and the wages are better than I had any reason to expect . . ." She bit her lip, ashamed of having mentioned this personal matter.

"The Chevaliers are all very well as people go. You don't have to tell me that. We have always known the family, and the parents and grandparents — I grew up with the old man, who had a stroke and died last year, the day of the village fête. So you see! And there's nothing stuck-up about them either — Chevalier's just like his old man, always ready to drink a glass of wine with anyone. And as for food — if you stay there you'll soon put on some weight. No offense meant, of course, but you're not what I'd call fat. . . . But you won't stay, you poor little soul."

"But why won't I stay?"

The train had stopped at a small station. There was no one on the platform except a porter, who was unloading a basket of chickens and an empty barrel from the baggage car.

"Why won't you stay? Has anyone said anything to you about the Terror?"

"The Terror?"

"Yes. Your pupil, Ernest."

"I was warned that he was a difficult child. . . ."

Loucrocq roared with laughter. "Difficult! That's a good one. Tell me, Mademoiselle — it *is* Mademoiselle, isn't it?" he asked with sudden formality. She gave a slight shrug and answered curtly: "Yes."

"Well then, Mademoiselle, do you know how many governesses the Chevaliers have had in the last three years? Seventeen, no less! And the last one left the morning after she arrived. You see what I mean?"

"I know how to control children. It's my job."

"Control Ernest Chevalier? What a hope! Listen, have you got a return ticket? No, of course not. Pity! If only we had met at the station in Bordeaux I would have told you to buy a return ticket. Do you know what you had better do? Stay in the train: it leaves again at nine o'clock and you can be back in Bordeaux by midnight. The eighteenth governess won't even have got off the train. That will be really something!" He guffawed again and once more slapped his thighs.

The governess answered drily that she was not to be frightened off. But her next remark showed that the words had struck home.

"All difficult children are very much alike. What makes your Ernest so different from the others?"

"Different! He's different all right! He's in a class by himself. Nothing I could say would give you the faintest idea what he's like. We'd be in Millasse long before I could tell you a quarter of the stories there are about

11

him. Just imagine a kid who has never heard the word 'no' from anyone since he was a babe in arms. Even his most stupid and dangerous pranks are forgiven. Listen to this: one day he decided he wanted to have his supper on the pigsty roof. And so for days on end he ate his supper on the pigsty roof. Two weeks ago last Sunday was the village fête, and he insisted on spending the whole day on the merry-go-round. Then in the evening he wanted to take one of the horses home with him. Naturally the owner yelled at him. But the Terror yelled even louder, as he can, until you could hardly hear the fairground music. In the end Ernest's father offered the man five hundred francs to unscrew one of the wooden horses and take it to the boy's room. It must still be there — he hired it for a month. But it will have to go back some time . . . if Ernest will let it go. If he won't, then his father will have to shell out again."

"But what sort of man is he, the father?"

"All this is because he lost his wife when Ernest was born. He and his mother-in-law — I shall have to tell you something about Madame Garrouste — have made the kid their whole life. You can't think what it's like. I'm telling you, Mademoiselle, they're mad. . . . Last month, for instance, it was still the closed season for game, Seconde — she's Ernest's nurse and thinks the world of him, as you can imagine — well, Seconde came to me and said that she absolutely had to have a partridge. So I told her the shooting season hadn't started. 'I know that,' she said, 'but young Master Ernest wants partridge for his dinner tomorrow. Madame Garrouste told me to pay whatever I had to.' Well, I do a bit of shooting myself, you know, Mademoiselle, and I didn't want to encourage poachers. But I've always served the family and they rely on me. And anyway I thought that I would get something out of it. So I got in the car and set off. But there's not much game left in this part of the country, only a few crows and squirrels, and it was getting on for evening before I came across a wood-cutter who told me he knew of some. He promised he'd have a shot at a partridge early next morning and bring it to me on his bicycle. When I got back to the shop, there were Monsieur Chevalier and old Mother Garrouste wanting to know where the bird was. When they heard there *might* be one the next morning you should have heard the way they carried on. 'What *will* the child say? He's been sulking all afternoon as it is — and now he'll see us come home empty-handed! We shall have to tell him we left it in the butcher's icebox.'

"By ten o'clock next morning my partridge still hadn't arrived. Old Garrouste and Seconde were wait-ing in the back shop wailing about having told the kid they'd got his partridge and wondering what would happen when he found out. 'Well,' I told them, 'you'll just have to spank him, won't you?' At that point the man arrived with the partridge. But that wasn't all: he told us the police had been after him, and you won't believe it but we had to pay him eight francs for the bird to make it worth his risk. And then there was an-other four francs for me. Then we all set off together to take the Terror his partridge. We found him in the garden, riding pick-a-back on young Gaudran, the draper's boy. Kicking him quite viciously he was, too. Madame Garrouste called out: 'Here's your partridge, darling,' but he just went on digging his heels into young Gaudran and shouting 'Gee-up!' and never even looked at the partridge. 'Look at the pretty birdie, my precious . . . Would you like it roasted, on a spit, with lots of lovely butter?' Now you'll never believe this, Mademoiselle, but that little devil just turned on us, his face scarlet with fury, and yelled: 'I don't want partridge — I want sausages!' "

Loucrocq slapped his thighs again, tears of laughter streaming down his fat cheeks as he repeated: "Sausages! He wanted sausages! . . . You can imagine, with tricks like that — and there's no end to the stories I could tell you — his family has had just about enough."

"Have they never thought of sending him to boarding school?"

"Indeed they have! They think of it every year. They enter him for a different school each time, but then, when he's due to go, the little devil is always ill, though he's as fat as butter. But that's just it: he eats too much. Stuffs all day long, he does, so of course his insides are always upset. Then his family gets worried and the upshot is he doesn't go. Anyway, as his father says, no school would ever keep him. And he's not yet eleven, so you can imagine what he'll be like when he's older. There's nothing anyone can do with him."

He was still talking, but the governess was hardly listening. Clearly she had been misled. Tempted by the offer of a high salary, she had turned down other posts which would be filled by now. But perhaps the fat butcher was only trying to frighten her? Perhaps he was exaggerating? After all, it might be fun to show these country bumpkins how Mademoiselle Thibaud could handle a difficult child.

"Ernest is under eleven, after all," she said, "he's just a little boy . . ."

"A little boy!" Loucrocq interrupted her. "Why, he's bigger than you are! His size is as unnatural as his temper. Would you like to know why the last governess left within twenty-four hours? Because he kicked her in the shins, that's why. Oh, yes, he can be tough — he's as strong as an ox, and there's no holding him when he loses his temper. Do you know why the governess before last left? She had locked Ernest in his room, so he upped and jumped out of the window — the second floor, if you please. Luckily he fell into a flower bed. She caught the next train . . ."

"So shall I."

This time Mademoiselle Thibaud seemed to be convinced.

"You'll be the first to leave without even *seeing* the Terror. Perhaps this will make the Chevaliers realize it's time to do something drastic. But whatever you do, don't tell them I told you all this. Say you heard people talking on the train, people you didn't know. They know everyone talks about Ernest. But it wouldn't be nice to put me in their bad books when I've done you a good turn. I don't want to lose their custom, see! So watch your step."

Mademoiselle Thibaud did not answer; she was thinking. It was already late in the year and the only jobs left unfilled were those no one wanted. She had already used nearly all her savings. The Chevaliers had certainly treated her unfairly, but then it was up to her to have found out more about the job.

"On second thought," said Loucrocq suddenly, "you had better stay long enough to get your month's money in compensation — he can't eat you, after all."

The governess replied that she was not the sort of person to cheat her employers, once she had made up her mind to leave.

"*They've* cheated *you* all right, haven't they? Here's Millasse now, and I can see the Chevaliers' car headlights. Well, shall I get your luggage out or not?"

Hunger made up Mademoiselle Thibaud's mind for her. Surely there must be dinner waiting for her? There would still be time to catch the train afterwards. It would not hurt her to see the Terror. Perhaps he was not as terrible as the butcher had made out.

$\mathcal{T}wo$

The village was already asleep as the car drove through it and, once past the last houses, in through a pair of tall gates. In the glow of the headlights, Mademoiselle Thibaud saw a long, two-storied house flanked by a pair of dumpy outbuildings. Her heart thumped as she climbed the front steps and entered a damp, tiled hall pervaded by a smell of cooking fat. A servant in a black head-scarf took the luggage from the driver and greeted the governess.

"You must be hungry, Mademoiselle. Supper is ready. If you'd like to wash your hands first . . .".

Her initial hunger was already satisfied by soup and stuffed cabbage by the time duck and green peas appeared on the table. The woman in the black head-scarf who had welcomed her filled Mademoiselle Thibaud's plate, despite her protests. She was younger than the governess had at first thought, but her toothless mouth and shrivelled lips made her look like an old woman.

"You are very kind, Madame . . . er . . . ?"

"Seconde. Just call me Seconde."

"Ah, you are Master Ernest's nurse?"

Seconde looked at her in surprise, and said suspiciously: "Well now, who could have told you that?"

Mademoiselle Thibaud had drunk two glasses of the excellent white wine with which the nurse plied her, and she felt in splendid spirits, ready to face anything.

"I should like to speak to your master and mistress."

"I don't think they'll be able to see you this evening."

"Have they already gone to bed?"

Seconde did not answer at once. She looked uncomfortable.

"I suppose you could see the master — at least, if the Terror goes to sleep quickly."

"What Terror? Ernest?"

"Yes. The poor child is ill, you see. His tummy's upset . . . he ate too much lamb for lunch. So of course his father can't leave him until he goes to sleep. Master Ernest wouldn't have that."

"What about Madame Garrouste?"

"Oh, you certainly can't see her until tomorrow."

"Has she already retired, then?"

"Dear me, no. She sleeps with Master Ernest, because whenever he's ill either his grandmother or I have to pretend to be ill, too. He's no ordinary boy, you know. If he's not better by tomorrow morning I shall take Madame Garrouste's place in bed, and if he has to have a laxative then I shall have one, too. Perhaps I shouldn't be telling you all this, but you may as well be warned. He's not a bad boy at heart. Just a bit spoilt."

"A bit spoilt indeed!" echoed the governess. But Seconde was impervious to irony.

"Well, will you please inform your master that I wish to speak to him this evening."

"I can try — but if Master Ernest isn't asleep. . ."

Mademoiselle Thibaud did not have long to wait. The nurse came back with a message that Master Ernest did not seem to want to go to sleep and her master was playing checkers with him: he looked forward to meeting her in the morning.

"This evening or not at all," the governess broke in sharply. "Unless I have an interview with your employers immediately, I shall take the first train."

"Now, now, do you think you're the mistress here?" exclaimed Seconde, shocked.

Mademoiselle Thibaud replied that she had no desire to be either mistress or maid: all she wanted was to go away. Seconde threw up her hands in horror: "Go away! But you've only just arrived! Whatever's the matter with them all! You haven't even seen your pupil. He's not a monster, you know. I dare say you have been hearing wicked stories—people are so ill natured!"

The governess did not deny having overheard on the train a few remarks about Ernest which had left her very little wish for a closer acquaintance. This made Seconde highly indignant. According to her, the people who were most malicious about Ernest were the very ones who could not bring up their own children properly. The Parentis in particular, she said, would do better to hold their tongues.

"My sister-in-law was in service with them and let me tell you that she can remember their little boy one day trying to — yes, exactly! All over the roast that was on a spit over the fire . . . And he must have been three or four years old at least. The whole family were begging him to be a good boy and do it somewhere else. Now, you may not believe me, Mademoiselle, but our Ernest has never done such a thing — never! Besides, I wouldn't let him, not me. Ah, here's the master now."

A tiny, bald-headed man with a potbelly and heavy, purple jowls had just come into the room. His eyes were round with perpetual astonishment, and he had full, greasy lips. He was dressed in a maroon dressing-gown and carpet slippers.

"She wants to leave, sir," Seconde burst out.

"Who wants to leave?"

"Why, the young lady, to be sure!"

The little man's eyes grew rounder than ever and he drew himself up with dignity. "Is this a joke, may I ask?"

Mademoiselle Thibaud looked him straight in the eye and told him that her mind was made up.

"But this is not playing fair with us! It is hardly the conduct we expected from someone with your excellent references. . ."

"I am sorry, but it was you who induced me to come here on false pretences by failing to warn me I was to be entrusted with the education of an infant Nero."

"An infant Nero?" Monsier Chevalier was appalled.

"Yes, a young monster."

"I forbid you to abuse my son like this," screeched the little man. "He is the victim of small-town gossip. He has a complex character, that is all, and like all complex characters he is a little difficult. The vicar was saying to us only last Sunday that he is like a thorough-bred horse — difficult to break and never bridled."

"A runaway horse, I should say!"

Chevalier was repeating: "A runaway horse!" in a

shocked voice when there was a shrill cry from upstairs. "Papa! Papa! Papa!" The little man listened.

"Answer him," begged Seconde.

"No. I told him I was going to the — well, he mustn't know I am here."

The three of them stood still and listened. They heard a whining voice punctuated by another, milder one. Monsieur Chevalier's anger seemed to have evaporated. He glanced at the governess, who was looking up at the ceiling with a sardonic smile. Suddenly he appeared to take the plunge and broke out:

"Well, yes, you are quite right: he *is* an infant Nero. I still think there is some good in him, but tomorrow may be too late. You are our last hope. If you desert us we are lost. Everything we have heard about you makes us certain that you alone can save this unhappy child, and us with him. You can't desert us! Must I go down on my knees to you?"

At this point the door opened to admit an old woman, also in a dressing-gown, who looked as though she had just got out of bed. She was wearing loose slippers, and her sparse grey hair was scraped into four skimpy pigtails. Madame Garrouste had the same round, astonished eyes as her son-in-law, although they were not related by blood. Hers, however, were watery and heavy-lidded.

"Has he let you come down?" exclaimed Seconde.

The old lady put a finger to her lips. "Sssh! He mustn't hear us talking. Yes, he let me come because he wants to see the young lady, of all things!"

"Wants to see her?"

"I think he really is afraid of being sent away to school this time. He wants to see whom he has to deal with."

Mademoiselle Thibaud watched in amazement as Monsieur Chevalier turned to Seconde and said: "Tell Madame Garrouste that the young lady wants to leave tomorrow morning."

Seconde, calmly acting as interpreter between two people who spoke the same language, repeated to her mistress: "The young lady wants to leave by the first train tomorrow morning."

Still speaking to Seconde, Ernest's father added: "Say she heard people talking about Ernest. . ."

Seconde repeated for Madame Garrouste's benefit: "She heard people talking about Ernest. . ."

Perhaps the old lady was deaf? Yet the servant was not raising her voice, or placing any particular emphasis on her words. Mademoiselle Thibaud said: "Nothing I may have heard before makes the slightest difference. What I have seen and heard since I have been in this house is quite enough."

Suddenly Madame Garrouste begun shuffling about the room, huddling, like an old rat, against the walls and moaning softly: "She wants to go already . . . and she hasn't seen anything! Good Lord, what have we done for people to be so unkind? After all, he does want to see you. You can tell he isn't really bad! It's nice of him . . . he wouldn't do as much for everyone."

"Suppose you form your own opinion," put in the

boy's father. "It can't do any harm to talk to him. Who knows, you may even like him . . . especially if he's in a good mood. But I suppose that would be too much to hope for."

"He can certainly get 'round a body when he feels like it," said Seconde. "He has a way with him."

More than ever determined to escape, Mademoiselle Thibaud still felt a prick of curiosity. However, she also felt bound to warn Monsieur Chevalier that, although she would be happy to meet Ernest, nothing would alter her decision. At this, the pantomime was repeated while Ernest's father instructed Seconde to suggest that Madame Garrouste go and prepare Ernest for his visitor. The servant conveyed the message to her mistress and the old lady answered:

"Tell your master that it would be better if we both went up together."

The strange pair, who communicated entirely by means of an interpreter, went out together. Madame Garrouste told Seconde that three knocks on the ceiling would be the signal that she could bring up the governess.

As soon as she was left alone with the nurse, Mademoiselle Thibaud asked the reason for her employers' extraordinary behaviour.

"It has been going on for two years now," Seconde told her calmly. "Yes, it was two years ago last Michaelmas they quarreled about something—I can't remember what. Oh, yes, that was it! When the master has ortolans for dinner he puts the whole bird in his mouth at once and then puts his hand over his face and no one must speak to him while he is eating. He says the slightest noise disturbs his enjoyment. But there's no living soul who could stop Madame Garrouste talking . . . so of course they quarrelled. And because neither of them will take the first step, they've never made it up."

"For two years!" Mademoiselle Thibaud could hardly believe her ears. Seconde shrugged.

"That's nothing. The old lady's husband is dead now, but she went for eighteen years without speaking a word to him. And they were never out of one another's sight. Even when old Monsieur Garrouste was dying he told the sister who was looking after him in the hospital to tell his wife that he had always loved her just the same. I know because she told me. And his wife was there at his bedside all the time, poor thing. They kissed each other but they didn't say a word . . . as if after sulking for so long it wasn't worth the trouble! Madame Garrouste used to say to me: 'The funny thing is, Seconde, we can't remember any more how it all began . . . we had the quarrel in 1884 or '85 . . .' I think she rather likes not speaking. The fact that she is doing it again with her son-in-law proves it, though her tongue can wag fast enough with the tenants and servants. But that's because they'll listen to her and always agree. The master is just like her: they both want everybody to agree with them. You can understand it, can't you, with all that money?"

Just then there were three knocks on the ceiling.

"That's the signal! Now, whatever happens, don't be afraid. He can't hurt you. And he can be very sweet sometimes . . . not often, but you never know. Perhaps he'll take a liking to you. When he does take a fancy to anyone, he does it properly — he can't bear them out of his sight."

"That's all very well, but supposing he takes a dislike to me?"

"Hmm, that's quite likely," Seconde said, looking the girl carefully up and down. "He doesn't like people to look shabby. It's just one of his fancies. . ."

With these encouraging words, she picked up an oil lamp from the hall table and led the way up the worn, linoleum-covered staircase. Mademoiselle Thibaud followed, suddenly shivering with cold — and with fright.

Three

Many years later, Mademoiselle Thibaud could still re-
call her first impressions when she opened Ernest's bedroom door that evening. It was a big, untidy room, lit
by a tall lamp standing in the centre of a round table
near the bed. The wooden horse from the fairground
stood on the carpet, huge, fixed in its motionless gallop,
decked out with velvet and gold spangles and with a
brass plate on the top of its head. From shadowy
corners and the tops of cupboards peeped a host of
animal heads — a whole, expensive menagerie of giant
sheep and goats. A model theatre stood by the window,
its gold trimmings gleaming in the dark, and the small
bodies of the puppets lay strewn about the floor. On
the big table, an army of lead soldiers was in rout amid
a scene of carnage where the model railway tracks had
come apart, overturning the carriages and spilling the
engine on its side.

Mademoiselle Thibaud had just started towards the
bed when suddenly a bulldog leaped up from beside it
and slipped between Monsieur Chevalier's legs, barking
furiously. He succeeded in grasping and holding it by
the collar, but the dog continued to growl and bare its
sharp teeth.

"Make Dingo lie down, pet," begged Madame Garrouste, looking at the bed. "He won't obey anyone but
you. Call him."

The boy who, up to this point, had been invisible, sat

27

up and stared at the governess who had beaten a strategic retreat to the door.

"Call him off, darling," echoed Monsieur Chevalier. "I can't hold him much longer. Help me, Seconde."

But the darling in question maintained an Olympian calm while Seconde helped her master to restrain Dingo by petting him and soothing him in a dialect of her own.

"We'll have to shut him up in the scullery," she threatened.

Ernest did not sound perturbed. "I won't let you. Dingo is going to stay right here tonight."

He had not taken his eyes off his new antagonist, and she returned his gaze. As far as she could judge, the child was already far too fat. He had his father's heavy jaw, but his jet-black hair was thick, his small nose aquiline and his wide, rosy mouth a good shape. All in all he would have been an attractive child but for the sour, prematurely adult expression. The governess wondered whether there was anything more depressing then the sight of a child so spoilt that he had nothing left to wish for. The fierce look he gave her almost made her quail: he must be sizing up his unknown adversary's strength. Still, at first sight she rather liked him.

Suddenly he disappeared without warning underneath the bed-clothes and turned his face to the wall. All that could be seen was a hunched figure, a mop of black hair and the pink tip of one ear.

"Say good evening to Mademoiselle Thibaud, darling," wheedled Madame Garrouste in honeyed tones.

Seconde took up the refrain: "You must say good evening to the nice lady, or she won't stay here and then you'll have to go away to school."

But Ernest stayed as still as a mouse. Then his father moved a step nearer the bed and, drawing himself up to his full height — which was not much — said:

"Ernest, I am asking you, and if necessary I will order you to say hello to Mademoiselle Thibaud."

The two women reacted to the temerity with terrified admiration. But the invisible hump did not budge.

"Shall I give you a nice present then, sweetheart, if you'll be a good boy?" said Madame Garrouste. "Listen to Granny, now." With a mixture of coaxing and threatening she began to chant: "Does little Ernest want a hamster? Well, he won't have a hamster if he's not a good boy! Does little Ernest want a live snake? Well, he won't have a live snake unless he's a good boy!"

Mademoiselle Thibaud could not stop herself breaking in: "Does little Ernest want a six-legged calf, then . . ."

The boy's father was just beginning pettishly: "May I ask what you mean by that?" when the hump stirred and a cross voice from under the tumbled sheets said:

"If I want a hamster I shall have one! And if I want to breed snakes and put them in your beds . . ."

"Ernest!" wailed Monsier Chevalier.

Mademoiselle Thibaud merely remarked under her breath: "Delightful child!"

A tousled head emerged abruptly from the bed-clothes, and Ernest shrieked: "What's the matter now?

Are you all trying to stop me from going to sleep? This is my room, isn't it? Surely the house is big enough for you to leave me in peace!"

"We shouldn't have upset him," said Madame Garrouste.

The infant Nero squatted on his bed and stared at his slaves. "Seconde, stay with me till I go to sleep, but don't let me hear you moving, or blowing your nose, or breathing . . . You can take Dingo out." With this, he turned back to the wall.

His nurse sat down meekly on a chair beside the bed and remained stock-still. Chevalier, Madame Garrouste and the governess went down to the dining room without a word.

"Seconde will come and help you unpack," Madame Garrouste ventured timidly, "as soon as he has gone to sleep."

"That will not be necessary, thank you. I shall catch the eight o'clock train. All I ask is that you be good enough to have my luggage taken to the station."

"You can't mean this?"

"You aren't going to desert us?"

Each seized hold of one of the governess's hands and clung to it.

"I'll double your salary," cried Chevalier. "This is madness, but I'll double it."

Mademoiselle Thibaud answered coldly that she would not stay for three times the amount. Madame Garrouste buried her face in her hands.

"Then this is the end of us," she moaned, "the end. I

can't stand any more. I have a weak heart. Nothing but a broken-down old windbag, that's all I am. And what do you think my poor son-in law will do, left all alone with such a terror?"

The governess suggested that the child might become better behaved as he got older and, failing that, they could always try boarding school.

"It would have to be an approved school to keep him," said Monsier Chevalier. "Poor Ernest, he's the most to be pitied. And it's all my fault — yes, my fault!"

Without warning, the little man burst into tears, screwing up his face like a child while the big drops rolled down his sagging cheeks. His mother-in-law began to wail in chorus, beseeching the Lord to tell her what they had done to deserve such misery. Then Seconde appeared and added her share to the hubbub.

"Oh, lordy, lordy! And to think the young lady won't even try. Some people . . ."

"Listen."

The wailing stopped and three anxious faces turned to Mademoiselle Thibaud.

"There may be a way . . ."

"Whatever you say!"

But Mademoiselle Thibaud shook her head and murmured: "No, you wouldn't hear of it."

"At least tell us!"

"No, you'd never agree to it."

"I'll agree to anything," cried the little man. "Do you want still more money?"

Mademoiselle Thibaud said it was not that: she had had an idea, but they would think it ridiculous.

"It can't do any harm to tell us."

The governess looked thoughtfully at Monsieur Chevalier's tearful baby face, and then at the two women, Madame Garrouste wagging her head idiotically, Seconde clasping her work-worn hands tightly together. The governess was not a hard woman but, used as she was to taking orders and to frequent humiliation, she enjoyed the feeling that, for once in her life, she was the person on whom the situation depended: it was her turn to grant the favours now. She turned to Monsieur Chevalier.

"You have another house, haven't you?"

Yes, he told her, a country cottage at Brousse, twenty-five miles away. "In fact if it weren't for Ernest we would be there already, for the shooting. But Ernest doesn't like shooting: he hates sitting still; he must always be on the move."

"Well, this is what I have to suggest: you leave here tomorrow morning and go to Brousse, taking Madame Garrouste and Seconde with you. I will stay here with Ernest."

"Alone? Leave Ernest without his father or me, or even his nurse — you can't be serious!"

"You see, Madame, you think it's out of the question. But that would be the only way."

"Why is it out of the question?" put in Monsieur Chevalier. "I agree with Mademoiselle Thibaud: she will achieve nothing as long as we are here."

Suddenly Seconde understood. She began to wail: "What? Leave my lamb? Leave him all alone with some strange woman? You'll have to drag me away by force, then."

"Quiet, you old fool!"

But she would not be quiet, and soon Madame Garrouste was adding her own cries to the uproar.

"He's used to us, poor child. Who will dress him in the morning, and cut his bread, and peel his fruit? Who'll see he doesn't catch cold?"

The governess took no notice of these protests, and began questioning Monsieur Chevalier about the staff.

"The tenants look after us at Brousse — they are famous for their cooking — so we can leave Emily, the cook, here with you, and the maid, Augustine. And then there are people in the village who will come in and do the heavy work."

"No," moaned Madame Garrouste, addressing an imaginary audience. "He can't do it. He can't leave the poor child my daughter entrusted to him on her deathbed . . ."

"We've got on very well without the young lady up to now," shrilled Seconde. "Let her catch her train! We won't run after her. Here's this complete stranger with her city ways coming here and queening it over the master and mistress . . ."

But Monsieur Chevalier had taken the governess aside and was saying: "I am beginning to see exactly what you mean, and your plan gives me confidence precisely because of its boldness. All three of us will leave tomorrow morning, and we won't come back until you think fit."

"He has taken leave of his senses!" wailed Madame Garrouste. "Seconde, tell him so." But Seconde was past hearing. She was keening softly to herself: "Ah, the poor wee moppet!" She could hardly have made more fuss if Ernest had been dead. Ignoring this, her master told her to go and pack his and her mistress's things.

"But actually leaving will be the most difficult part," he added to the governess. "Ernest will make a dreadful fuss."

"There will be no fuss if you leave quietly, before he wakes up."

"What! Without kissing him goodbye?"

"I am asking this sacrifice of all of you. Can I rely on one of the men to keep the gate shut and stop the boy from going out without my permission?"

It was Seconde who answered: "Oh, yes, you can rely on them. Castagnet can't bear the child; he'll be only too glad to help you torture the poor wee thing."

Monsieur Chevalier propelled the nurse towards the door. He was in the grip of a delicious excitement. What a release! He would be free to shoot his wood pigeons in peace.

"You shall have the house to yourself at eight o'clock tomorrow morning, I promise you, and then you can set to work."

It was only when she was alone in her own room that Mademoiselle Thibaud realized what she had undertaken. Monsieur Chevalier believed she possessed some infallible method of dealing with difficult children. In actual fact she had no method, and no plans. She had not done badly so far in separating the infant Nero from his slaves, she reflected. Now she was alone, face to face with the monster. But what method should she use to tame him? Force? Gentleness? Cunning?

She opened the window and breathed in the smell of the autumn night. The moonlight fell on a few ancient oak trees, a clump of sage brush near the stone steps and a sanded walk. Dingo, in the scullery below, was growling in answer to the crazy barking of the village dogs. In a little while they had all stopped, and there was only the crowing of the cocks.

"Living all alone in this great barracks with that little horror . . ." thought Mademoiselle Thibaud. After all, the worst that could happen to her was failure. He would not eat her. She might even manage to take him in hand. There must be some way to his heart. Yes, that was the main thing: to find the way.

"All the same," she reflected, "he will need very firm handling to begin with. He won't take easily to being curbed. Still, it might be interesting . . ."

She dozed off, and when she awoke the early light was filtering through the shutters. "The first thing to do," she thought, "is to put a wire grill over his window at once."

She got up, dressed quickly and went downstairs.

Four

A car engine was purring outside the front door. Ernest opened his eyes and turned over. In his dream the car was about to start and his father was going for a drive without asking him to go, too. Was it really the car, or Seconde's voice, or Granny's maybe? No, he was decidedly not dreaming: that was really the car shifting gears as it gathered speed, and he could hear Seconde squawking like a flustered hen.

With half his mind the Terror was angry, but the other half simply wanted to go to sleep again. It would do his father no harm to wait. Ernest did not allow anyone to have a good time without including him. He shut his eyes again.

An odd noise woke him: as though someone was hammering on the wall outside his window. They must be taking down the dining-room blinds, he thought. They couldn't even let him sleep in peace now! "I'll take it out on them for this," he promised himself.

The hammering was getting louder. Laziness, with the youngest member of the Chevalier family, was an even more deep-rooted vice than bad temper, and Ernest did not move. All the same, this was too much. Then it began to dawn on him that, unlikely as it seemed, the racket was going on right beside him, just outside his room.

He jumped out of bed, hauled back the curtains and opened the shutters on the inside. Then he rubbed his eyes. A solid wire grill was already nailed firmly to the window frame, and there was Lanosse, the village lock-smith, unhurriedly descending the ladder.

"What's going on?" Ernest was so surprised that he forgot to scream. He rang the bell. Seconde was never far away. But no one came. The house seemed curiously silent. He opened the door and ran out on to the land-ing in his bare feet, calling furiously for Seconde. It was the housemaid, Augustine, who answered.

"Your breakfast is coming up."

"I wasn't talking to you."

The Terror went back to bed, shaking with fury. Seconde would come soon and then he was going to have something to say to the old hag! Just then he realized that Dingo had not come and scratched on his door as he usually did, and he rushed back to the win-dow and shook the grill wildly.

Someone knocked on the door — that was not like Seconde or his grandmother — and a thin, mousy-haired stranger came in carrying a tray. The governess.

"That's not your job," Ernest told her rudely. "Go and get Seconde, and hurry up about it! What's that, anyway? Coffee? I always have chocolate too, so that I can choose."

The governess ignored this outbust and put the tray on the bedside table.

"You won't be having chocolate any more," she said. "It's too rich for you. You are going on a diet, starting today. I want my pupil to be healthy."

For a moment Ernest was too astonished to speak, then he gasped: "Who . . . who is the boss here?"

"I am," she answered calmly.

"You?"

He was kneeling, white-faced, on the bed, his jaw set and an angry glint in his eyes. "This is a fine way to start. I'll tell my father — he'll teach you to say you are mistress here."

"I am aware that this will be a shock to you, my poor child, but he has given me complete authority. You must be reasonable . . ."

The boy did not answer. He was listening: there was still the same odd silence about the house. He glanced at the grill.

"What about that? Who dared . . .?"

"I did. To make sure you don't leave this room except by the door."

Ernest leaped out of bed and made a dash for the stairs, yelling for his father, his grandmother and Seconde. No one answered. He came back and gasped:

"Where are they?"

"Gone."

"For the whole day?"

"For as long as you take to become a good boy."

She would have been happier with tantrums than with the sullen, brooding silence that followed.

"I suppose you think you will win?" he said at last.

"I have no wish to *win*, as you put it, Ernest, I merely want you to be a normal, happy boy."

"I shall be happy when I've got rid of you, and that won't take long. I'll start by staying in bed, and I won't get up until you get out."

"You'll have to be very brave to starve yourself to death, Ernest."

"Who told you I was going to starve to death?"

"Well, if you won't come downstairs to the dining room . . ."

"I shall have my meals brought up here."

"Let me tell you, boys of your age do not give orders; they obey them."

"We'll see about that."

"We have seen already. Your meals will be served in the dining room at the proper times, and that includes breakfast from now on."

"So if I won't eat them, I shall starve?"

"It hasn't come to that yet, my lad. But supposing it did, we should have to resort to forcible feeding."

Ernest suddenly realized that he was actually being lured into talking to this horrible woman. He lashed out at the breakfast tray with his fist: there was a crash of breaking china, and milk and coffee poured over the floor. Then he turned his face to the wall and pulled the sheet over his head.

Mademoiselle Thibaud took no notice. She took a folded piece of paper out of her pocket. "Here is your daily timetable," she said. "Seven-thirty: get up, do your exercises, dress and say prayers. Eight o'clock: breakfast, playtime, and then lessons until ten. Then a walk. Lessons from eleven to twelve, lunch and a rest period until two. Lessons until three. Another walk, and lessons until tea time. Five to six: lessons, playtime, and private study from six to seven-thirty. Supper and a little reading or conversation before bed at nine o'clock. I'll put this timetable on the mantelpiece and I shall expect you in the schoolroom shortly."

As soon as the door shut behind her the Terror sat up and began to think. He would not get the better of this one as easily as the rest. Most of the time his tempers were not real, only put on to terrorize his family and get his own way. The governess's indifference to them robbed him of one of his most powerful weapons; he would have to find another.

Augustine came in without knocking, picked up the broken china and mopped up the spilt coffee and milk with a cloth. At the same time she was watching Ernest out of the corner of her eye, surprised to find him so calm.

"Bring me some more breakfast, at once."

"Oh no, not two breakfasts, Master Ernest. You won't be able to eat your lunch." Only when she had almost reached the door did she dare add: "Besides, Mademoiselle Thibaud has given strict orders."

There was silence once more. Ernest, who had never been alone in his life, felt nervous, almost frightened. He got up again, opened the door gently and leaned over the banisters, calling softly: "Dingo." Then, louder: "Dingo! Dingo!"

They must have taken the dog with them. He always jumped into the car when it started. Ernest was alone, quite alone; but he would show them who was stronger. She would not dare let him starve to death . . . All he had to do was stay in bed. Then he would get up in the night and raid the larder: there was always plenty of food there. He'd show them.

Five

Loucrocq was in his shop, holding forth to the assembled village gossips. "Oh yes," he was saying, "even in the train I could see at once that little bit of a thing knew what she was about. She's packed them all off: father, grandmother and Seconde, and she's the mistress there now. She knows what she wants, too. Madame Lanosse can tell you: that governess was there at six o'clock this morning asking Lanosse to make a wire grill to put over the boy's window. Augustine told me that took the wind out of the lad's sails: he doesn't even scream any more. He won't get up, but he's stopped screaming. She'll tame him like a bad dog — by stopping his food. And she'll train him! She may look skinny, but she's tough."

"It may be as you say, Monsieur Loucrocq," said Madame Gaudran, the draper's wife. "But I would never leave *my* boy at the mercy of a strange woman I knew nothing about. I say we should all keep our eyes open to make sure nothing happens to the poor innocent. The papers are full of such stories. There are so many dreadful crimes, I've always wondered why I've never come across one. I'd be only too glad to give evidence in court. Ah well, I'll tell you what I think: I shouldn't be surprised if no good comes of it. What's that grill for, I should like to know? To incarcerate him?"

"To what?" asked Loucrocq. "The words you use!"

"That means shut him up," explained Madame Gaudran. "It happens even in the best families, you know; people are shut up in the dark, without food or drink, and the police find them lying in their own filth."

Madame Lanosse agreed with her. "Quite true, Madame Gaudran. There must be something wrong with strangers, I always say, or why don't they stay where they belong? This woman must have come to Millasse because she's got something to hide. You won't make me think any different."

"And how do you explain the way she has managed to get rid of all the family so quickly, Monsieur

Loucrocq? It looks very peculiar to me. She must have put a spell on them."

"This isn't the Middle Ages," protested Loucrocq. "There are no witches any more."

"No more witches! What about the one at Gazinet? And the witch at Jouanhaut who got rid of my three warts? No more witches, indeed! I'm telling you," Madame Gaudran finished up, "Ernest is the apple of their eyes. The Chevaliers would never have gone away of their own accord. It's not natural. *I* say we should keep an eye on this little nobody. And witch or no, is that how the Chevaliers want their boy brought up? They have enough property and investments to do as they like. Is it any of that young woman's business? What does she think she's doing, interfering like that, anyway?"

Loucrocq, always anxious to please his customers, said quickly: "Oh, it's nothing to do with me. It does me no good to have the Chevalier house shut up and the Terror starved, when he used to eat enough meat for four because he can't stand vegetables. There aren't very many houses in Millasse where they eat meat twice a day. Yes, the more I think about it. . . . I hadn't reckoned on being out of pocket. So if she thinks we'll stand by and let her make a martyr out of the Terror. . . . After all, we're all very fond of him at heart. He's one of the curiosities of Millasse!"

As soon as she got home, Madame Gaudran sat down at the counter of her little draper's shop, took a large sheet of lined paper and wrote,

45

My dear Seconde,

It has not been long before I have some bad news to tell you. This is to warn you that the news is as dreadful as it can be. Madame Lanosse and I have found out that this woman has put a spell on the Chevaliers (I can't imagine how you escaped becoming a victim yourself, you poor dear. They must have had to carry you away by force)! Can you imagine that in this enlightened age there are still monsters who would lock up an innocent child and keep him without food? Yet that is what is happening in your house, and that nasty Augustine admitted to Loucrocq that your poor little Ernest was already so weak he could not cry out, and can't leave his bed.

This is to let you know everyone in Millasse is very worried about him, and we all think the police will be called in soon. That is all there is to tell. By the way, you have not paid me yet for the buttons and laces you bought last Wednesday, though of course I am not writing to remind you, because naturally I trust you implicitly.

Your lifelong friend,

ELODIE GAUDRAN

P.S. Call in at the shop on your way home, if you manage to persuade your employers to return. You ought to have a witness, in case you catch the witch torturing poor little Ernest.

Six

Before she sat down to dinner that evening, Mademoiselle Thibaud stood at the foot of the stairs and listened intently, but no sound came from Ernest's room. She took her place a little anxiously opposite the empty chair in the huge, dank dining-room. She must stand firm whatever happened.

"You are sure you took everything out of the larder?" she asked Augustine.

"Yes, Miss. I have taken everything down to the cellar, including the jam and preserves and the hams, just as you ordered. There isn't a crumb for a mouse to nibble."

The maid poked the wood fire that blazed in the hearth. She was a strapping, coarse-featured girl and she was laughing as she spoke because she detested the Terror.

"Well, on second thoughts, leave a piece of bread and cheese on the kitchen table. Have you told the child supper is ready?"

"I went right into his room, but he had his face turned to the wall."

"Did you tell him there were roast duck and parsnips, and a tart?"

"I even told him there would be a bottle of his father's wine — he drinks like a man already, you know."

"And he didn't budge?"

"Not an inch."

"We'll wait and see."

The governess managed to appear calm in front of Augustine, but in fact she was beginning to worry. She decided to keep watch all night instead of going to bed.

About eleven o'clock she heard a door opening upstairs. She hid underneath the stairs by the cellar door and saw Ernest walk past within arm's length, but he did not notice her. He held a candle and had wrapped a red bedspread around him. With his bare feet, his handsome, rather pudgy face and bright, feverish eyes, he really did look like an infant Nero — a small Caesar, kept a closely guarded prisoner in his own palace.

He went down the passage and straight to the larder. Then he stifled a cry: it was empty. There was not so much as a meat bone or a crust of bread. He looked up, but there were no hams suspended from the beams and no pots of preserves on the usual shelves.

The boy stood still in amazement, listening to the autumn rain pattering on the roof and in the gutters. Then his famished gaze took in the table where a piece of bread and some Gruyère cheese stood in full view. They were obviously put there out of pity by the enemy, and for a second or two Ernest managed to resist them: this frugal meal was the final insult. But he could not hold out for long, and started to eat ravenously.

He was just swallowing the last mouthful when he heard a whimper outside the garden door. An animal was whining. "Dingo!" he called softly, and was an-

swered by a small bark. In an instant the boy had the bolts drawn and was tugging at the heavy door. Dingo hurled himself at his master — a soaking wet, muddy Dingo, but Ernest did not notice it. The bedspread slid to the ground and he hugged Dingo tightly, shivering in his pyjamas and letting the dog lick his face all over.

While he was rubbing the dog's neck he felt a small package fastened to his collar. It was a letter, folded up tightly, and he recognized Seconde's childish handwriting. Ernest tore open the envelope and read it.

My dearest boy, my own darling chick, I know Dingo will bring you this letter because he is much cleverer than many people. It is to let you know they took your Seconde away by force and your poor Granny is ill with grief. But the master is so happy shooting his pigeons that he has forgotten all about his little boy. If you are very miserable, I hope you will manage to escape somehow. Go to Madame Gaudran. She will take you in and feed you. I was able to slip in a word to her before I left. Your loving nurse,

SECONDE

"Not likely!" muttered Ernest. "If she thinks I'd go to that old Gaudran. . . ."

He thought for a moment. He had lost the first round, that was clear. He would have to retire, like a good general, in order to counterattack more effectively.

Feeling comforted by the presence of his dog, Ernest

decided to go back to his room, but Dingo was lying in a corner, still whimpering pitifully. He must be hungry, but there was nothing for him to eat except a few crumbs left on the table. Dingo sniffed them and then, to his master's surprise, lay down again without touching them, though he did empty his bowl of water greedily. When the dog stood up to drink Ernest noticed a patch of blood on the ground where the poor creature had been lying. There was more blood on his pyjama jacket. He grabbed the candle in terror and bent over Dingo, and soon found a deep cut on his hindquarters. The dog was panting and still whimpering softly, as if he were asking his young master to help him.

Ernest, who was used to being waited on hand and foot, lost his head and began bawling at the top of his voice. He broke off suddenly when he realized that the enemy had come into the room and was standing holding a lamp. Seeing the boy's bloodstained pyjama jacket, she thought at first that he had been hurt, but she had hardly moved before Ernest said: "It's not me! It's Dingo! He's dying. . . ."

Dingo. She breathed a sigh of relief and examined the dog who, far from trying to bite, obviously regarded any human as a potential saviour. She filled a bowl with water and washed the wound with her handkerchief, and then cut away the blood-matted hairs with a pair of scissors.

"Go on washing the wound, Ernest. I have something in my room to dress it with."

As she went light-heartedly upstairs Mademoiselle

Thibaud bumped into Augustine, who had been awakened by Ernest's shrieks. In a few words she told her what had happened and asked her to go down to the cellar and get Dingo some milk and something solid to eat.

When she came down again she was carrying a bandage, some adhesive tape and hydrogen peroxide, and in a few deft movements had completed the dressing. Ernest sat still on a chair, wrapped in his red bedspread. The governess went out into the passage for a moment and he heard her whispering to Augustine. Then she came back with a bowl of milk which Dingo drank thirstily.

"He is feverish," she said. "His nose is hot. We'll put him in your room. You take the lamp and go on ahead." She picked up Dingo like a baby and carried him upstairs, while Ernest went first to light the way.

When the procession reached the bedroom they found a reluctant Augustine just finishing laying a table beside the bed. On it were some cold ham and chicken, a slice of tart and a bottle of wine.

"This will help you to get over the shock," said Mademoiselle Thibaud.

She made the dog comfortable on a cushion and put a rug over him. "He licked me," she said.

But now that the Terror's first anxiety was over, he was determined not to answer. He merely sat down and started eating without looking at the governess again.

When he had finished, she cleared the things away

herself. "You shall have your breakfast in bed tomorrow morning because it will do you good after such a late night. Good night, Ernest."

A grunt was the only answer, but even this was better than nothing. The town hall clock struck one, and silence reigned once more in the Chevalier household.

The governess, however, was not asleep. Hope was keeping her awake, though she made an effort not to give way to it. The game was not yet won, and the most important part was still to come. But she no longer felt alone: something had occurred, unsought by her, which had made contact between herself and her pupil possible.

Seven

When the governess entered Ernest's room at nine o'clock the next morning with his breakfast tray, he was kneeling on the floor beside the dog.

"He's better," he called out. "His nose is cold."

Then, suddenly remembering, he let his face fall into its old sulky lines. Mademoiselle Thibaud felt her heart thumping as she said:

"As soon as you are dressed you can take Dingo into the garden before you come to the schoolroom for lessons."

"You'll just have to wait for me," he said with an attempt at bravado.

"Certainly, Ernest. I shall wait as long as is necessary."

She waited in vain until lunchtime.

When Ernest came into the dining room the governess was already in her place, with a book. She did not look up and did not speak a word to him during the meal. Deliberately he ate noisily, banging his glass against his plate and dropping his knife, but nothing aroused the slightest sign of interest in the enemy.

Nevertheless, if Ernest could have seen the dismay which lay beneath Mademoiselle Thibaud's apparent calm, he would have been triumphant. She wondered if she would have to resort to stopping his food again, forbidding him wine and dessert until he would do his lessons. She was prepared to fall back on these harsh measures, but she had to try another way first. But what? For want of a better idea she decided to write him a letter, appealing to his intelligence and finer feelings and painting a dreadful picture of his probable future. Mademoiselle Thibaud made up her mind to write the letter that very afternoon, so that he would find it on his pillow when he went to bed. Then she reflected that he would not read it. His first impulse, she was sure, would be to tear it up; he would merely see it as a sign of weakness, of giving in; but all the same she meant to try again. The main thing was to provoke discussion between them.

She let her thoughts run on, while the rain rattled on the window panes of the small study where Augustine had lighted a fire. This little room was separated by the dining room from the drawing room, where Ernest was amusing himself by picking out tunes on the piano. He relied mainly on one finger, but occasionally attempted an accompaniment with his left hand.

When Augustine brought in the afternoon post, the governess asked: "Does he take music lessons?"

"That's a good one! He doesn't take any sort of lessons. But when he feels like it he'll spend days on end at the piano, getting on everyone's nerves, because I must say that's one thing the master can't stand. He's always saying music is the most irritating sound in the world. The Terror's got all sorts of toys, but have you noticed he hasn't a gramophone? The master has forbidden anyone to mention them to him, but he does know that

they exist. Children are funny. He's never thought of
asking for one, and yet music is about the only thing he
really likes. The only place he'll sit still for a second is
in church — on account of the singing."

He certainly has talent, thought the governess. One
had only to listen to the sounds improvized by those
small, searching hands to be sure of that.

The rain stopped, and the sun drew Ernest out into
the garden. Mademoiselle Thibaud had an idea: it
wasn't a very good one, she thought, but it was worth
trying. She went quickly through the dining room, and
saw that the boy had left the french windows in the
drawing room open. Then she sat down at the piano.
The instrument was a fine Erard, but it had evidently
not been tuned for some time.

She played a Chopin prelude first, then another, pay-
ing much less attention to the music than to the sound
of cautious footsteps outside. She did not look 'round,
but she was sure someone was listening. She could feel
someone there. This was already an achievement: the
Terror had been drawn by the very first bars.

Would he come into the room? He resisted the impulse for a quarter of an hour, and the governess was
beginning to lose hope when she heard him at last. No
sooner had he sat down in an armchair near the window
than Mademoiselle Thibaud stopped short, closed the
piano abruptly and stood up.

"Why have you stopped?"

She turned round and looked at the boy sternly: his
face was red and his eyes devoured her.

"Well, you don't really expect me to play for you, do you?"

"You can't stop me listening. And anyway, it's my piano!"

"That's as may be, but I shall not play any more."

"Never?" he asked desperately.

"If you were prepared to do some work, I would play at the end of every lesson; but since you won't work . . . And in the evenings after dinner, I would play whenever I was pleased with you . . ."

"Play for me a little longer; then I'll come and work."

She looked at her watch. "It's after two o'clock. Remember your timetable: you have lessons until three. But then, if you have tried to be good . . ."

He clenched his fists. "No! Now! This very minute!"

"An hour will go very quickly, Ernest, and I have so much to teach you."

She moved towards the door. Ernest was still shouting furiously: "Now!" but she did not turn around.

"You will find me in the schoolroom," she said.

She sat down at the inkstained table, opened a book, sharpened a pencil, and waited. She did not have long to wait. Sniffing rebelliously, hands in his pockets and shoulders hunched, the Terror came at last.

Epilogue

"It's just as I tell you, Madame Garrouste. Augustine has not bought any meat from me for two days now: she is boasting that the young lady is taming the Terror by starvation, like a wild animal."

"Like a wild animal! Loucrocq! And when I think that Monsieur Chevalier wouldn't come with us!"

"Oh, when he's out shooting," cried Seconde, "they could make mincemeat of his poor child and he would never turn a hair. Let's go to the house at once; at this very moment she may be beating him."

"I'll come with you, as a witness," announced Madame Gaudran. "Are you coming, Monsieur Loucrocq?"

"Give me a second to take off my apron."

Madame Gaudran suggested leaving the car in the square. "Otherwise she'll hear us coming and we won't be able to catch her red-handed."

The town hall clock was just striking one. Loucrocq and the three women walked along the road leading to the Chevaliers' house. Madame Garrouste groaned with the effort of keeping up with the rest of the party. They went in through a side door opening on to the lane, and Dingo came rushing to meet them. He did not bark, but he flung himself on Seconde in transports of delight.

"There you are, then, you poor creature! Well now, you're hurt; you're wearing a bandage. Has she been ill-treating you too, you poor dog?"

"Be quiet, Seconde," said Madame Gaudran. "The young woman will hear us."

The little group crept, cat-footed, into the hall. Someone was playing the piano in the drawing room.

"That must be her. . . . She's probably locked the poor child in the cellar and now she's enjoying herself!"

"No, not in the cellar, surely!" wailed Madame Garrouste.

The dining room door was open and they risked a glance inside. The remains of a meal were still on the table.

"Well, there are two places, I will say," remarked Loucrocq quietly.

"They've had a tart and stewed fruit, too," added Seconde. "Look at the plates."

"It may not have been the Terror who ate with her," Madame Gaudran hinted. "She's mistress here, after all; she's probably inviting all her friends."

But Madame Garrouste had already unfolded Ernest's grubby table napkin. "Oh dear me, this is my Terror's all right. I'd know it anywhere. There's no one like my poor darling for messing up his napkin. If you looked all over the country," she went on, lyrically, "you wouldn't find anyone capable of dirtying the table linen so fast."

Somewhat disappointed, Madame Gaudran suggested that they should go into the garden and look through the window to see what was going on in the drawing room. They followed her along the side of the house to the open french window and, once there, they had no need to hide. The governess was sitting at the piano with her back to them, with Ernest in a chair beside her, absolutely still. Seconde noticed that for the first time in his life he had a straight part in his hair and a clean shirt collar.

Madame Garrouste could not contain herself any longer: "My darling! My poppet!"

Mistress and pupil looked 'round in surprise. The Terror was the first to speak.

"What are you doing here? Now you've interrupted! Go on, please, Mademoiselle Thibaud. You promised."

"Ernest, is that the way to welcome your grandmother and Seconde? Go and kiss them nicely, now."

He obeyed, grudgingly enough, but he obeyed. The governess, however, said to Madame Garrouste coolly: "There is something you have forgotten, I suppose?"

"We just came in because we were passing," the old woman stammered.

"Just to see . . ." Seconde added nervously.

"We are leaving again at once," Madame Garrouste finished hastily.

"You may stay with Ernest during his playtime. He does not begin lessons again until two o'clock."

"But what about the music?" wailed the boy.

"I will play after supper this evening. We won't read for as long as usual."

"But we were going to finish the second chapter of *Oliver Twist!*"

"Well then, we'll go to bed a little later. On condition that you are nice to your granny and Seconde," she added in an undertone. "Monsieur Loucrocq, was there something you wanted?"

"Nothing at all, Mademoiselle. Or, at least — just to bring you the congratulations of all Millasse. I told them you were no weakling and they shouldn't judge by appearances."

The butcher made his escape without waiting for an answer and caught up with Madame Gaudran by the garden gate.

"Well, you put your foot in it, all right, Madame Gaudran."

"Put *my* foot in it!" she protested irritably. "Do you think it's perfectly natural for the Terror to change like that, from one day to the next? I tell you, she's put a spell on him. You won't make me think any different, and it will all come to a bad end, you'll see. You'll remember what I told you. We shall have trouble here yet!"

"That's very likely, Madame Gaudran," Loucrocq agreed heartily.